Anne Fine

*The HAUNTING *of* Uncle Ron

with illustrations by
Vicki Gausden

Barrington Stoke

For Joseph

First published in 2014 in Great Britain by
Barrington Stoke Ltd
18 Walker Street, Edinburgh, EH3 7LP

www.barringtonstoke.co.uk

Text © 2014 Anne Fine
Illustrations © Vicki Gausden

ISBN: 978-1-78112-285-3

Printed in China by Leo

Contents

Chapter 1

Spooky!

There I was, staring out of the window.

We had new people moving in next door and there was a girl. She looked AY-MAY-ZING in her bobble hat and stripy socks. And she looked nice as well.

Then I saw a taxi stop outside our gate, and Uncle Ron got out.

Uncle Ron is the sort of visitor that no one wants. He doesn't warn you he's coming. He just arrives on your door step with two giant suitcases, and beams at you.

"Surprise!" he says, as if everyone should be happy to see him. "Surprise!"

And it's not a nice surprise, either.

Uncle Ron never says how long he plans to stay. He's always stuffing his face. He has three meals a day when he's here, and he eats non-stop snacks. He leaves crumbs on the kitchen counters, and he brews strange herbal teas until our tea pot stinks of things like fennel and rose hips. Uncle Ron thinks that someone else will wash and iron all his clothes without so much as a "thank you" from him.

And he spends all day talking to old, dead people.

"What?" I asked Mum one morning. "Uncle Ron really talks to ghosts and ghoulies?"

"No," Mum said. "No one as interesting as that. Just boring old dead people." She saw the look on my face. "He talks to spirits, Ian," she explained. "Shades from the other world. People who have 'passed over'. People who are dead."

I gave a little shiver. "Spooky! What do they want?" I said.

"Just listen in," said Mum. "You'll find he chats to them about where he may have left a missing sock. Or whether the red spotty tea-towel might have fallen behind the fridge. Or if his best blue underpants are in the wash."

"Why would a spirit bother to come back from the Other World to chat to Uncle Ron about something as boring as where he might have left his socks?" I asked.

"Search me," said Mum.

"But have you heard these spirits talking?" I demanded.

"Of course not," Mum said. "They're just in his head. The problem is that Uncle Ron has no imagination. That's why his chats to all the people in the Other World are about dull things like missing socks, instead of something interesting like missing bodies, or the looming threat of plague, disaster or death."

Chapter 2

A Shade from the Other World

So I took Mum's advice and listened in.

I hid behind the door while Uncle Ron was having one of his non-stop snacks. A jam sandwich this time. He dipped his knife into the jam and all of a sudden he lifted his head.

"Is that you, Mrs Hall?" Uncle Ron asked the air. "Are you trying to get in touch with me?"

(I hadn't heard a thing.)

"I'm listening," he said to nothing and no one. "You're coming over to me loud and clear. What do you want to tell me?"

(Mrs Hall couldn't have been coming over that loud and clear. I still hadn't heard a whisper.)

"Really?" Uncle Ron said, as if he were astonished. "Yellow! I don't believe it!"

I waited.

Silence.

"No!" Uncle Ron said again. "How amazing!"

He chatted on for a while.

"Really?" he said. "And when was that? ... No! You astonish me! ... Good heavens!"

I'd no idea what Mrs Hall was telling him until much later, when we sat down for supper. (Well, not Mrs Hall of course, because she's dead. But all the rest of us.)

Dad started up by asking Uncle Ron what he'd been doing all day. (Apart from snacking.)

Uncle Ron clasped his hands together and beamed. "Such a good day!" he said. "I had a nice long chat with Mrs Hall. She is a Shade from the Other World. She's one of my favourite Spirits. She always has some interesting news."

"Oh, yes?" said Mum. "What did she tell you this time?"

Uncle Ron leaned across the table. "It seems the Spirit of Mr Potter, one of her oldest friends, joined her yesterday."

"You mean he's popped his clogs as well?" asked Dad.

"Passed over to the Other World," Uncle Ron corrected him. "And he told Mrs Hall that there are brand-new people living in her old house. And guess what!"

"What?"

"What?"

"What?"

(We were all agog.)

Uncle Ron told us the news. "These brand-new people have painted Mrs Hall's old front door. And now it's yellow!"

Dad kept his face straight. "No!" he said.

Mum chimed in. "Really?" she asked.

I wasn't going to be left out. "I don't believe it!" I shouted, a bit too loudly.

"Yes!" said Uncle Ron. "It's astonishing, isn't it? And Mr Potter said that there's to be a brand-new knocker on the door too. But they haven't chosen it yet."

"I am amazed," Dad said.

"That's the last thing you'd expect!" Mum chimed in again. "Who would have thought it?"

"I will tell everyone at school!" I said. "They'll be astonished too."

I was teasing, of course. We all were, but Uncle Ron was far too daft to notice.

Then Mum picked up the big blue oven dish. "More pasta, Ian?" she said to me before she offered it to Uncle Ron. (She asked me first because once Uncle Ron has dug a serving spoon into a dish, most of it's gone.)

Chapter 3

The Spirits on the Far Side

"He has to go!" Dad wailed the next day. "I can't stand any more. Ask him to go."

"You ask him," Mum said. "He's your uncle, not mine."

But Dad can't ever ask Uncle Ron to go. Mum says it must be something to do with all the happy holidays he had at Uncle Ron's house when he was a child.

Dad did his best. He sat down next to Uncle Ron. "So, how's it going?" he asked.

Uncle Ron beamed. "Fine, thanks!" he said. "And, my word, that pasta you cooked for us last night was just the job."

"Good," Dad said. Then he tried to work himself a little closer to the goal. "Thinking of staying much longer?" he asked.

"Oh, you know me," said Uncle Ron. "I'm not a man for timetables and plans."

Dad took a long deep breath. And then he fluffed it. "Lovely!" he said. "Tara and I really enjoy it when you stay with us." He turned to Mum. "Don't we?" he asked.

Mum gritted her teeth and said, "Yes, Alan. Yes. We really do."

But Dad could see that Mum was looking daggers at him from safe behind Uncle Ron's back. With an evil look, she drew one finger slowly across her throat.

The next day Mum gave up on Dad and started on me. "You do it," she said.

I wasn't listening. I was watching the girl next door. She wore a ra-ra skirt and had her hair in cornrows, with glittery beads like a kid, but she *still* looked brilliant.

"Do what?" I said at last.

"Make Uncle Ron go home. The man is driving me mad. So make him want to leave," Mum begged me.

I spread my hands. "Like, how?"

"I don't know," Mum said. "Play him your music. Show him your computer games. Tell him about those books you're always reading about the Planet Splendoff."

That really hurt my feelings. "I thought that you were interested in the Planet Splendoff."

Mum blushed. "I was. Quite interested. For the first five or six books."

(It was my turn to blush. I'm on Book 18 now.)

"All right," I said. "I'll have a go. I'll talk to Uncle Ron."

I started off all nicely and politely. "Uncle Ron, don't all your neighbours miss you when you're away from your own home for so long?"

"I don't think so," said Uncle Ron. "They've never said as much."

"Oh, I bet they do," I said.

Uncle Ron shrugged. "Oh, well. One person's loss is another person's gain."

"Who's gaining?" I asked, stumped.

Uncle Ron gave me a hurt look. "Your parents," he said. "And you, of course."

"Oh, yes," I said. "Of course."

Next I tried a bit more cunning.

"That bedroom you're staying in is horribly damp," I told him.

Uncle Ron looked up, startled. "Damp? I hadn't noticed."

"But it is," I said. "Aunt May slept there one night and caught the worst cold ever. It was almost pneumonia."

"It doesn't feel damp at all," said Uncle Ron. "Not with that radiator blasting out heat."

"Damp can be a very odd thing," I warned him. "You can feel warm and cosy as toast, and still be getting dreadful rheumatism and pneumonia."

"I'll take my chances," Uncle Ron said cheerfully.

I tried a different tack.

"What about all the Spirits on the Far Side?" I said. "I'm sure it would be easier for them all to find you if you were back at home."

Uncle Ron looked puzzled. "I don't think so," he said. "If any Shades or Spirits are looking for me, Mrs Hall will tell them where I am."

"Oh, right," I said.

And that was it. I'd fluffed it, just like Dad. I gave up and went back to staring out of the window at the girl next door.

Chapter 4

A Long, Thin, Silver Ghost

That's where Mum found me, still staring out of the window.

Her eyes followed mine. "Is that the new girl next door? She does look nice. Why don't you go and say hello?"

"How can I just go up to her and say hello?" I asked.

"Easy," Mum said.

"It's not easy at all," I snapped. "I'd say hello to her. She'd say hello to me. And then the two of us would just stand there like dummies."

"Not if you'd thought of something else to say."

"Like what?"

"I don't know," Mum said. "You could ask her a favour, or something."

"A favour?" I was baffled.

"Yes," Mum said. "A favour. If this girl is as nice as she looks, she'll help you out with whatever you ask her to do, and then the two of you will just get talking."

"It sounds dead easy," I said bitterly.

"Yes, it does, doesn't it?" said Mum. "And that's because it is." She turned away and then turned back. "Talking of favours, how are you getting on with the favour you're doing for me? You know. The Getting-Rid-of-Uncle-Ron favour."

"Not very well," I said. "I'm working on it. But I need to think some more."

One of my thinking places is on the step. That's where Dad found me.

"Aha!" he said. "Are you sitting here hoping the girl next door will walk past?"

"No, not at all," I said. "I'm doing Mum a favour."

"You don't look as if you're doing anything at all," Dad said.

"That's where you're wrong," I told him. "Because I am. I'm busy thinking."

"Well, while you're busy being Mother's Little Helper by thinking, do you mind grating a lump of ginger for me? We're having stir-fry for supper."

"All right," I said. (I do love stir-fry.)

But as I sat there on the step, grating ginger for my dad, his little tease spun round and round in my mind. Those three words – "Mother's Little Helper". I could remember seeing them somewhere in fancy, loopy print.

Mother's Little Helper.

But where?

All of a sudden, I remembered. When I was very young, we had a plug-in baby monitor. It was called Mother's Little Helper. (You wouldn't be allowed to give it a name like that now. It's far too old-fashioned and sexist.) Mum and Dad used to put it near my cot so they could listen in on me. Then they would rush upstairs if I began to cry.

Of course, I grew out of my cot and the baby monitor. But when I was about seven, I found it again in a cupboard. And after that I used it to listen in on Mum and Dad. Sometimes I'd switch on the monitor and hide it behind the big fat biscuit jar that sits on the kitchen counter.

Then I would go upstairs, plug in the base and listen.

Once I heard Mum and Dad talking about how much I should get for my pocket money. Often, I heard them chatting about things they had seen on telly. One day they just droned on and on about what colour to paint the kitchen. Now and again I heard a bit of gossip about the neighbours.

But mostly I used to hear them moaning about me. I was untidy. They had to nag me to clean my teeth every night. It was annoying that I wouldn't eat tomatoes. On and on and on.

In the end I got fed up and shoved the baby monitor and its base back in the cupboard.

That was all years ago, but I was sure that Mother's Little Helper would still be there.

I heard the patter of footsteps and I looked up. The girl from next door was walking past. Today she was in silver boots and wore a shimmering scarf that looked a little like a long, thin, silver ghost floating along beside her.

And that silver scarf gave me my brilliant idea.

I put the grater and the ginger down and ran to say hello.

Chapter 5

A Phantom Drifting Past

The girl next door is called Hetty.

She's the same age as me. She's starting at my school next week. And she was happy to do me a favour.

In fact, she thought it would be a laugh.

We didn't push our luck. We practised for a while, and then we waited till my mum and dad went off on their next trip to buy more of the food we needed for Uncle Ron and his snacks. Just as the two of them piled in the car with their shopping bags, I tapped on Dad's window. "By the way, what's Uncle Ron's middle name?" I asked.

"You should remember that," Dad said, "because it's Ian. Just the same as yours."

I knew Uncle Ron's last name – Pollard – because he sometimes stays so long that his post is sent on to our house.

"Right," I said. "Well, don't you worry. Hetty and I will take good care of him while you're away at the shops."

Dad stared at me. But Mum let out the clutch. The car shot off with Dad still staring back.

"Bye!" I yelled, and I watched the car till it went round the corner.

After that, Hetty and I were ready to begin. I wiped the dust off Mother's Little Helper and put in fresh batteries. I plugged it in. The little green light came on at once.

"Good luck," I said to Hetty.

Hetty grinned and wound her floaty silver scarf around her neck and mouth, as we had practised.

"Ready?" I asked her.

"Yes. Ready!"

So I went downstairs to find Uncle Ron. As usual, he was in the kitchen, making one of his snacks. I kept my back to him and hid the monitor behind the bread bin. Then I switched it on.

There was a soft and shimmery rustling noise. It came from Hetty, who was upstairs, fixing her silver scarf around her mouth a bit more tightly.

It sounded spooky, like a phantom drifting past ...

I had to hide my smile before I left the room.

Chapter 6

A Voice from the Land of Shades

I listened from behind the kitchen door.

Hetty was brilliant! Her very first whispers
floated into the kitchen. They were a little
muffled, as if her voice was coming to us from
some other world. The world of Spirits and
Shades.

"I call to you, Ronald Ian Pollard!"

Uncle Ron jerked his head up from the bread he was buttering. "Who's that?" he said. "Who's that?"

The monitor only works one way, of course. Hetty couldn't hear Uncle Ron, so it was pure luck that what she said next fitted in so well.

"I am a Voice from the Land of Shades," she whispered in a spooky voice. "I call from the Great Beyond. And I come to you, Ronald Ian Pollard, to warn you of terrible danger."

"Danger?" Uncle Ron looked worried. "What danger, Spirit?"

"A terrible, terrible danger!" Hetty repeated. "You must leave this house at once."

I peeped through the half-open door. Uncle Ron had stopped spreading jam on his bread. He looked even more worried.

"Leave this house?" he repeated. "But why?"

Hetty pressed on. "It is not safe for you to stay here for even another day. You must trust me, Ronald Ian Pollard! We spirits from the

Other Side know all there is to know. And since you have been such a friend to Mrs Hall, I have been sent to warn you."

"Oh, cripes!" said Uncle Ron. He went dead white.

"Go now!" said Hetty. "At once!"

Hetty waited just a moment, and then she added something. We hadn't practised it, but it was rather good.

"Go!" she cried. "Go now! Or the first letters of your three names will spell out something far more dreadful than Ronald Ian Pollard."

Uncle Ron worked it out as fast as I did.

R.I.P.

That's what they write on gravestones. It means Rest in Peace.

Chapter 7

A Message from the Great Beyond

I helped Uncle Ron throw his things into his suitcases. He didn't even finish making his snack or brewing his rhubarb tea. He phoned a taxi company. "Come at once!" he told them. "Come as fast as you can!"

He wouldn't even wait inside the house. He stood out on the step and twisted his head this way and that until he saw the taxi coming.

"Thank goodness!" he cried. And then he rushed down the path, carrying one of his cases. I took the other one for him. The taxi driver put them in the boot.

"The train station, please!" said Uncle Ron. He turned to me. "Please say goodbye to your mother and father for me. Tell them something came up. I couldn't wait."

"I'm sure they'll understand," I said.

I waved him off. So did Hetty. And then we went inside to wait till Mum and Dad came back from the shops.

"Gone?" Mum said. "Do you mean it? Gone?"

"Gone," I repeated.

"Taken his stuff and not left anything behind?" she asked, just to make sure.

"Only one half-made jam sandwich snack."

Mum dumped her shopping bags down on the kitchen table. "I don't believe it!" she said. "It's the best news ever! I am over the moon!" She turned to Hetty. "You must help us celebrate. Please stay for supper." Mum pointed at the bags. "We'll need all the help we can get to use up this mountain of food, if Uncle Ron has gone."

Dad looked at me. "But how did it happen, Ian? What set him off? What made Uncle Ron decide to leave all of a sudden?"

"I think he had a message from the Great Beyond," I said. "A call from the Other World. It seemed to scare him. One minute he was buttering bread for his jam sandwich. The next, he was packing his stuff."

Mum took the last shopping bag from Dad and dumped it on the counter beside the bread bin. The bag was so full and heavy that it leaned over, and sent the bread bin sliding away.

There was the baby monitor. Its little green light blinked at all of us.

Mum looked at me. I looked at Mum.

"So," she said, with a grin. "Mother's Little Helper ..."

She winked at me and I winked back.

"Just what I said to Ian," Dad said. "He's Mother's Little Helper."

I winked at Hetty. Hetty winked at me. And then we went to her house so that I could help her fix her bike.

This "asking favours" business really works.

Chapter 8

The Spirits Are Invited

We still see Uncle Ron. He won't stay with us any more. There's a small hotel along the road, and we go there to visit him when he's in town. Mum and Dad often invite him for a meal. "Come for supper at our house tonight," they say.

But Uncle Ron shakes his head. "No, thanks," he says. He prefers to go with us to Pizza Palace or the Korma Curry Corner. All of us like it there.

At first we thought that Uncle Ron wouldn't stay with us again because he was scared of our house. (Nobody wants to Rest in Peace too soon.) Then one day Hetty and I walked to the hotel with a jar of Dad's best plum jam. (Mum said it would help the cook at the hotel with all of Uncle Ron's snacks.)

Uncle Ron wasn't in the hall. He wasn't in his room. He wasn't in the garden.

Then Hetty spotted him. He was in the kitchen with Mrs Bell, the hotel cook. Mrs Bell sat at one end of the table. Uncle Ron sat at the other. They were so busy talking that they didn't notice Hetty and me out in the garden.

The window was open, so we could hear what they were saying.

"No!" Uncle Ron said.

"I don't believe it!" said Mrs Bell.

There was a bit of a lull while no one spoke. Then Uncle Ron said to Mrs Bell, "Did you hear what Mrs Hall just told us?"

"Yes!" Mrs Bell replied. "Those new people in her house have painted the front door again. And this time it's green. I am astonished!"

There was another lull while no one spoke.

Then Mrs Bell said to Uncle Ron, "Now, that was amazing news. The brand-new door knocker has fallen off. Have you ever heard anything so odd in your life?"

"Never," said Uncle Ron. "It comes as a great surprise."

The two of them went on like that for quite a while.

Hetty grinned. "Look at them! So happy together, talking to the spirits."

"And to each other!" I said. "Shall we come back another time?"

We left the jam for Uncle Ron at the front desk. But Dad said that we should have taken it home with us. "That's my best jam," he said. "And I'm pretty sure that Uncle Ron will soon be married to a cook. He won't need my jam any more."

And Dad was right. Uncle Ron doesn't need our jam any more. His wedding is next week. We are all going, Hetty as well.

And I expect the Shades and Spirits are invited too.

Our books are tested
for children and young people by
children and young people.

Thanks to everyone who consulted on
a manuscript for their time and effort in
helping us to make our books better
for our readers.

Also by **Anne Fine** ...

How Brave Is That?

Tom's a brave lad. All he's ever wanted to do is work hard at school, pass his exams, and join the army. He never gives up, even when terrible triplets turn life upside down at home.

But when disaster strikes on exam day, Tom has to come up with a plan. Fast. And it will be the bravest thing he's ever done!

Gnomes, Gnomes, Gnomes

Sam's a bit obsessed. Any time he gets his hands on some clay, he makes gnomes. Dozens and dozens of gnomes. Funny thing is, Sam doesn't like to have them in his room. So they live huddled together, out in the shed.

But when Sam's mum suddenly needs that space, she says the gnomes will have to go. And so Sam plans a send-off for his little clay friends – a send-off that turns into a night the family will never forget!

www.barringtonstoke.co.uk

More **4u2read** titles ...

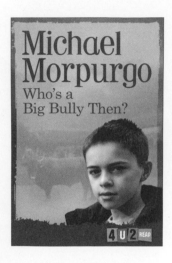

Who's a Big Bully Then?

MICHAEL MORPURGO

Olly is a bull. A very big bull.

Darren Bishop is a bully. A very nasty bully.

What happens when one of Darren's victims dares him to take on Olly?

Hostage

MALORIE BLACKMAN

"I'll make sure your dad never sees you again!"

Blindfolded. Alone. Angela has no idea where she is or what will happen next. The only thing she knows is she's been kidnapped. Is she brave enough to escape?

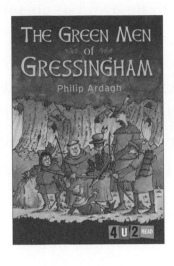

The Green Men of Gressingham

PHILIP ARDAGH

The Green Men are outlaws, living in a forest. Now they have taken Tom prisoner!

What do they want from him?

Who is their secret leader, Robyn-in-the-Hat?

And whose side should Tom be on?

The Red Dragons of Gressingham

PHILIP ARDAGH

The Green Men used to be outlaws. They lived in the forest and did brave deeds.

Now the Green Men are inlaws. They live in the forest and do ... not very much.

The Green men are bored. They need some fun. They need a quest ...

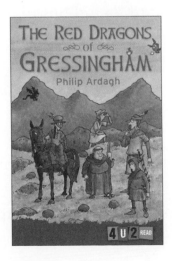

www.barringtonstoke.co.uk

At first we thoug
stay with us again b
our house. (Nobody
soon.) Then one day
hotel with a jar of De
said it would help the
of Uncle Ron's snack

Uncle Ron wasn't
his room. He wasn't

Then Hetty spott
kitchen with Mrs Bel
sat at one end of the
the other. They were
didn't notice Hetty a

The window was
what they were say

"No!" Uncle Ron's

"I don't believe it